WELCOME TO
PASSPORT TO READING
A beginning reader's ticket to a brand-new world!

Every book in this program is designed to build read-along and read-alone skills, level by level, through engaging and enriching stories. As the reader turns each page, he or she will become more confident with new vocabulary, sight words, and comprehension.

These PASSPORT TO READING levels will help you choose the perfect book for every reader.

READING TOGETHER
Read short words in simple sentence structures together to begin a reader's journey.

READING OUT LOUD
Encourage developing readers to sound out words in more complex stories with simple vocabulary.

READING INDEPENDENTLY
Newly independent readers gain confidence reading more complex sentences with higher word counts.

READY TO READ MORE
Readers prepare for chapter books with fewer illustrations and longer paragraphs.

This book features sight words from the educator-supported Dolch Sight Words List. This encourages the reader to recognize commonly used vocabulary words, increasing reading speed and fluency.

Enjoy the journey!

ABDOPUBLISHING.COM

Reinforced library bound edition published in 2018 by Spotlight, a division of ABDO, PO Box 398166, Minneapolis, Minnesota 55439. Spotlight produces high-quality reinforced library bound editions for schools and libraries. Published by agreement with Little, Brown and Company.

Printed in the United States of America, North Mankato, Minnesota.
092017
012018

THIS BOOK CONTAINS
RECYCLED MATERIALS

Licensed By:

LITTLE, BROWN

PUBLISHER'S CATALOGING IN PUBLICATION DATA

Names: Belle, Magnolia, author. | Berrow, Gillian M., author. | Hasbro Studios, illustrator.
Title: Pinkie Pie keeps a secret / writer, Magnolia Belle ; writer, Gillian M. Berrow ; art, Hasbro Studios.
Description: Reinforced library edition. | Minneapolis, Minnesota : Spotlight, 2018. | Series: My little pony leveled readers
Summary: Pinkie Pie learns the most exciting news in Equestria since Twilight Sparkle became a princess, but she can keep it a secret?
Identifiers: LCCN 2017943447 | ISBN 9781532140952
Subjects: LCSH: Leveled reader--Juvenile fiction. | Ponies--Juvenile fiction. | Secrets--Juvenile fiction.
Classification: DDC [E]--dc23
LC record available at https://lccn.loc.gov/2017943447

ABDO

Spotlight

A Division of ABDO
abdopublishing.com

MY LITTLE PONY

PINKIE PIE KEEPS A SECRET

Adapted by **Magnolia Belle**
Based on the episode
"The One Where Pinkie Pie Knows"
written by **Gillian M. Berrow**

LITTLE, BROWN AND COMPANY
New York Boston

Spotlight

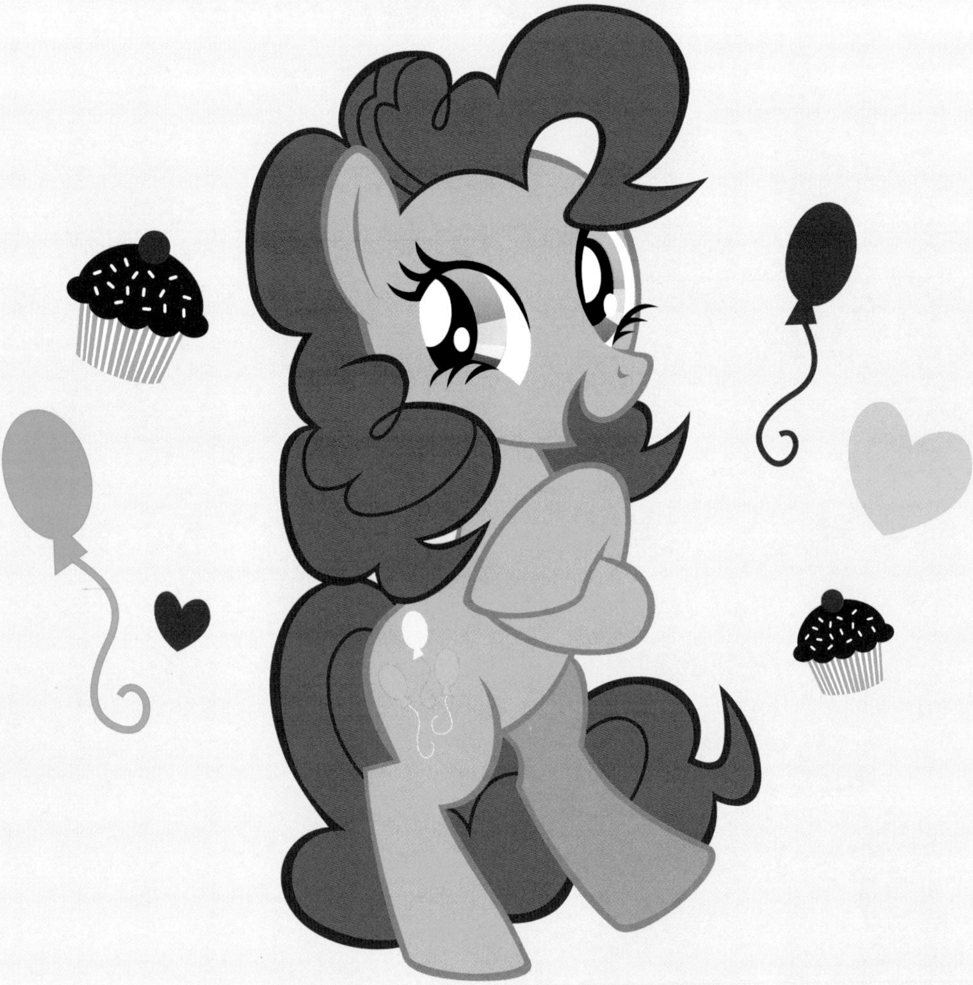

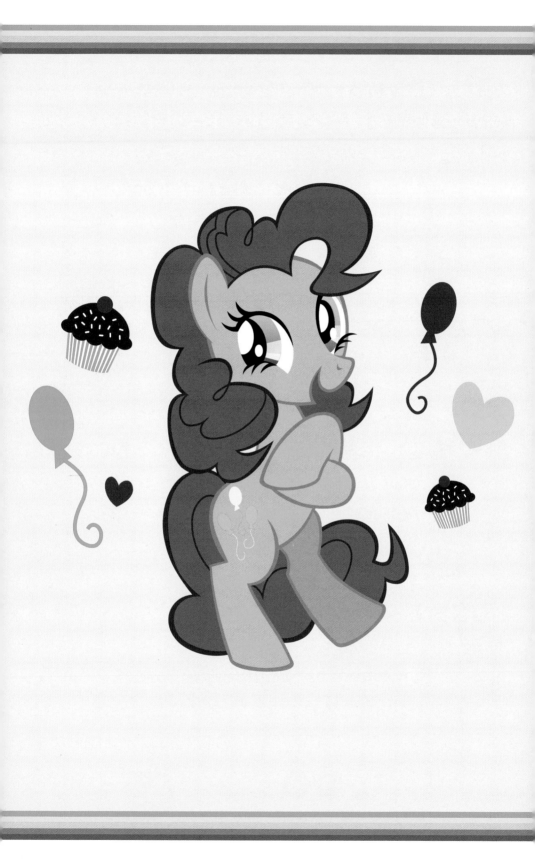

Attention, My Little Pony fans!
Look for these words when you read this book.
Can you spot them all?

cupcakes

disguise

snacks

certificate

Pinkie Pie is making cupcakes at
Sugarcube Corner when Mrs. Cake
gets a special letter.

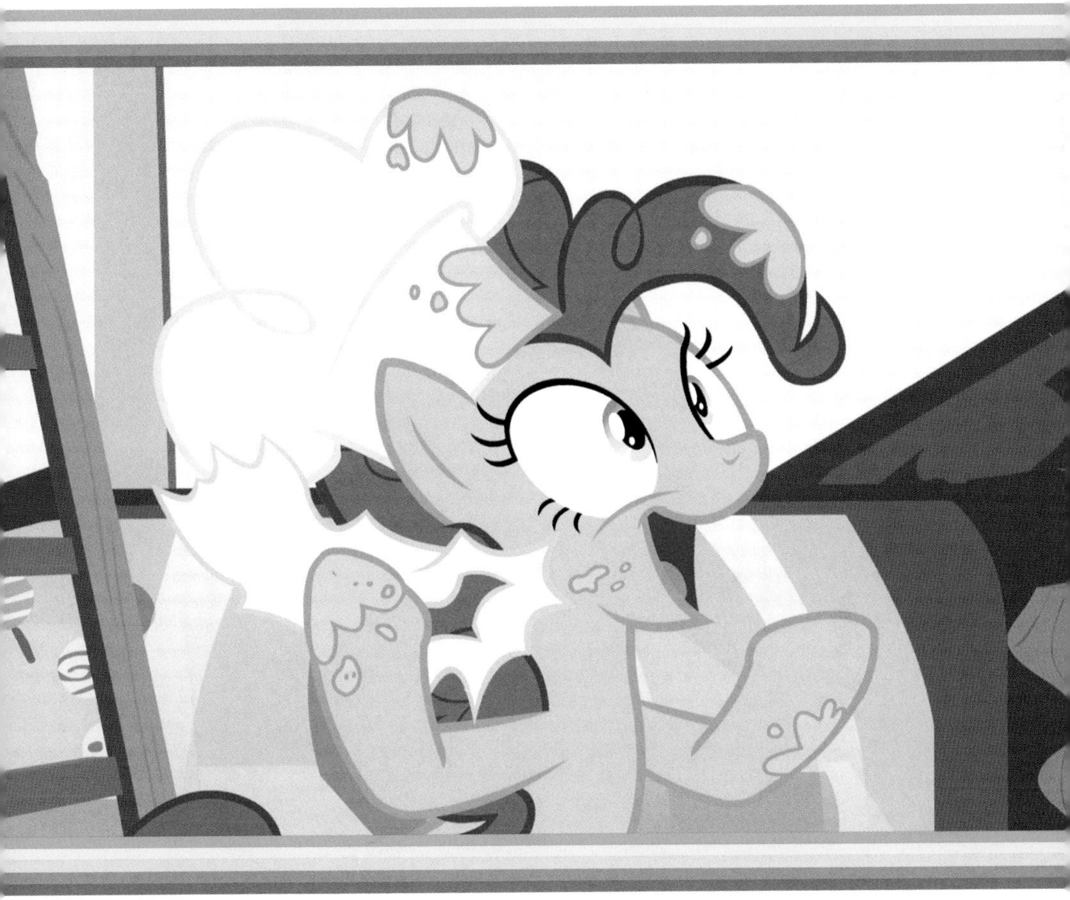

The letter says Princess Cadance and Shining Armor want a cake for their brand-new baby!

Mrs. Cake tells Pinkie Pie
that the new baby is a secret.
Pinkie Pie gulps.
"I have to keep a secret!"

Later, Pinkie Pie joins her friends
in Twilight Sparkle's castle.
The princess has news!

Twilight says that she is throwing a party for her big brother, Shining Armor, and Princess Cadance.

"And?" Pinkie Pie asks.

Twilight says that is all the news.

Pinkie Pie still has to keep the secret.

The friends decorate the castle
as a surprise for Shining Armor.
Talking about surprises makes
Pinkie Pie scared.
She is afraid she will tell the secret!

Twilight Sparkle finds a toy
that Shining Armor used to
play with as a baby.
Hearing the word "baby"
makes Pinkie Pie scared, too.

She asks the other ponies
if it is okay to tell a secret.

Rarity says no.

Pinkie Pie thinks she needs
to be alone to keep the secret.

Back at Sugarcube Corner,

Mr. Cake asks her to deliver orders.

Pinkie Pie is scared.

How will she keep the secret?

First, Pinkie Pie wears a disguise.
The Cutie Mark Crusaders can
tell it is their friend.
They ask if there is any news.
"Nope!" she says.

Next, Pinkie Pie sees Fluttershy.

She asks Pinkie Pie to bring snacks

like baby carrots to the party.

"Baby carrots?"

Pinkie Pie runs away.

Pinkie Pie decides the only way to keep a secret is to stay away from everypony.

Every time she sees another pony,
she zips by before they can say hello.

After she is done, Pinkie Pie is tired.

She still has to go to the party.

Pinkie Pie brings snacks
to the castle.
All the ponies are busy
getting ready.

Soon, Princess Cadance
and Shining Armor arrive
for the party!

Shining Armor has a game
for the ponies.
Twilight and her friends have
to find clues.
All the clues will reveal a surprise!

Shining Armor says that the first clue is "where young ones spend their week." The ponies think.

They find a clue in the schoolhouse!
It says to look at Applejack's birth
certificate.
Pinkie Pie dashes to the town hall.

The next clue says they need to "find a
place to buy comfy beds for little heads."
They need to find a baby crib!

The next clue tells them to "take a break where they can get a slice of cake."

The ponies go to Sugarcube Corner
and find Shining Armor and
Princess Cadance!
Princess Cadance tells Twilight to think
about what the clues have in common.

Twilight Sparkle looks at the clues: the schoolhouse, Applejack's birth certificate, a baby crib.

Twilight gasps!

 Princess Cadance and Shining Armor
announce, "We are having a baby!"

Twilight Sparkle asks,

"I am going to be an aunt?

That is the best surprise ever!"

Pinkie Pie is so happy.

"I did it!

I kept the secret!" she cries.

Everypony celebrates the good news
with cake!
Princess Cadance thanks Pinkie Pie
for keeping the secret.
Pinkie Pie laughs.
"Aw, it was a piece of cake."